OAK PARK PUBLIC LIBRARY
31132 012 559 088

W9-COL-384

Mooncakes

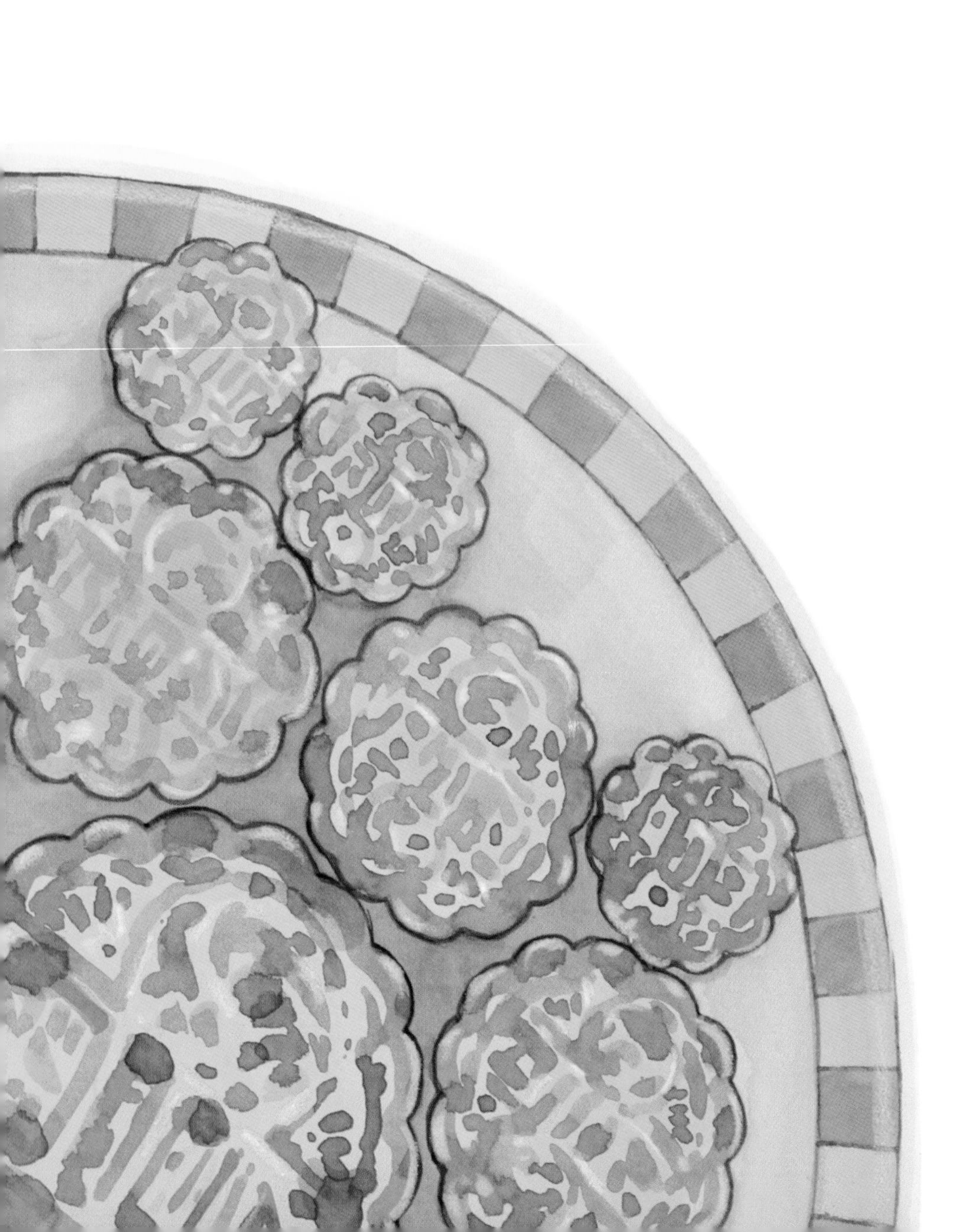

MOONCAKES

Loretta Seto

illustrated by Renné Benoit

ORCA BOOK PUBLISHERS

Library and Archives Canada Cataloguing in Publication

Seto, Loretta, 1976-
Mooncakes / Loretta Seto ; illustrated by Renné Benoit.

Issued also in electronic format.
ISBN 978-1-4598-0107-3

I. Benoit, Renné II. Title.
PS8637.E865M66 2013 JC813'.6 C2012-907458-6

First published in the United States, 2013
Library of Congress Control Number: 2012952944

Summary: A young girl shares the special celebration of the Chinese Moon Festival with her parents, who tell her ancient tales about Chang-E, the woman who lives on the moon; Wu-Gang, the woodcutter; and Jade Rabbit.

Orca Book Publishers is dedicated to preserving the environment and has printed this book on Forest Stewardship Council® certified paper.

Orca Book Publishers gratefully acknowledges the support for its publishing programs provided by the following agencies: the Government of Canada through the Canada Book Fund and the Canada Council for the Arts, and the Province of British Columbia through the BC Arts Council and the Book Publishing Tax Credit.

Cover and interior artwork created using watercolor, colored pencil and gouache.

Cover artwork by Renné Benoit
Design by Teresa Bubela

ORCA BOOK PUBLISHERS
PO Box 5626, Stn. B
Victoria, BC Canada
V8R 6S4

ORCA BOOK PUBLISHERS
PO Box 468
Custer, WA USA
98240-0468

www.orcabook.com
Printed and bound in Canada.

16 15 14 13 • 4 3 2 1

For my parents, Gaye and Barry Seto
—LS

For my family
—RB

Tonight the moon shines like a polished pearl, round and fat. It glows bigger and brighter than I have ever seen.

Tonight is a special night.

Tonight I am allowed to stay up late. Soon there will be mooncakes to eat, sweet and chewy. They are round like the moon. They make a circle for me and Mama and Baba. They make a circle for my family.

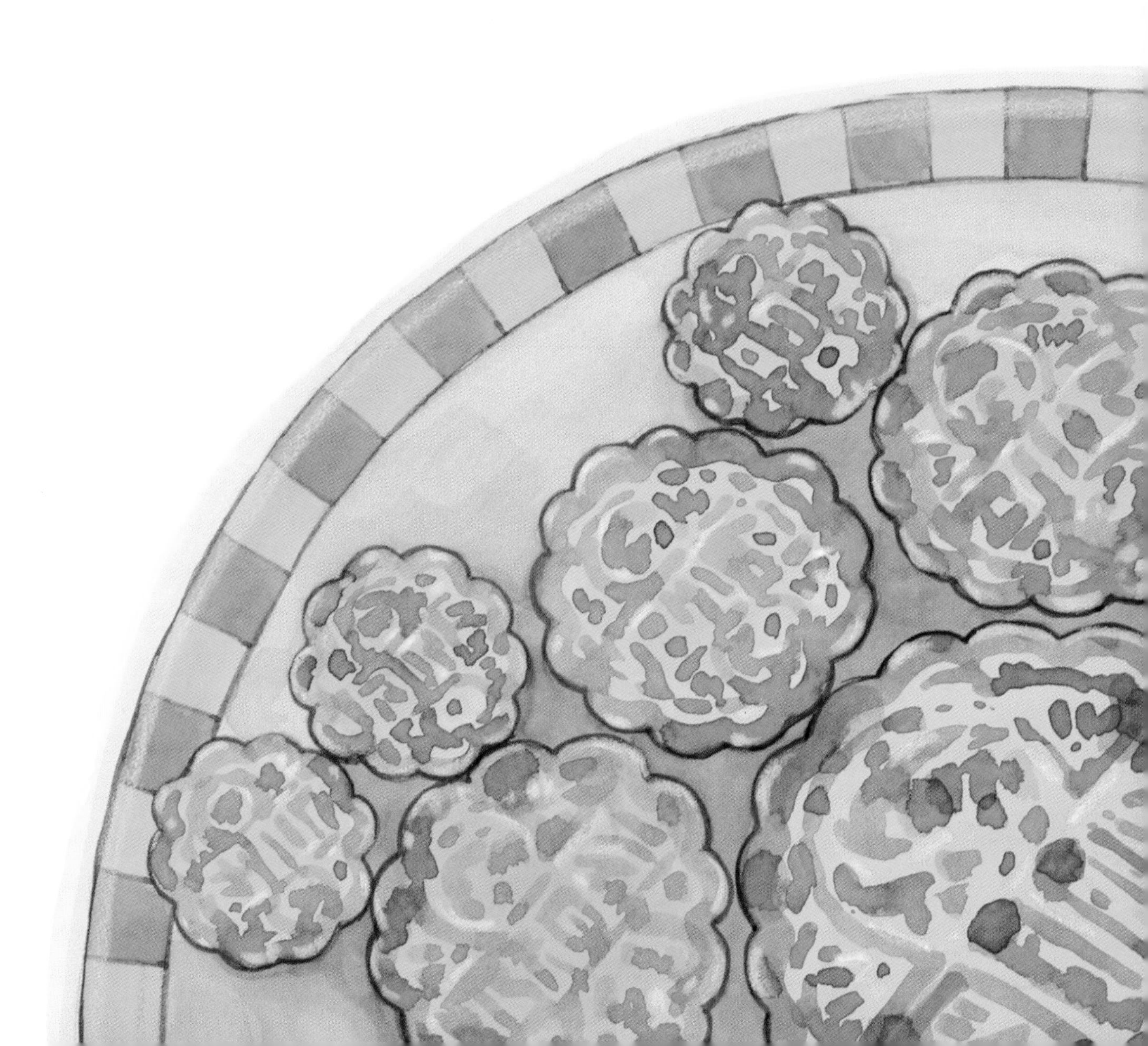

Outside, we light paper lanterns. I made one all by myself, using my favorite colors. The lanterns and stars light up the sky. The moon makes everything shine like silver and water.

In our backyard, we sit together in a big chair. We watch small, dusty clouds brush the moon's face. The wind shakes the leaves. *Husshh, husshh*. Baba pulls the blanket close.

Mama and Baba tell me about Chang-E, the woman who lives on the moon.

Long ago, the world had ten suns in the sky, and it became too hot and dry.

The Jade Emperor asked his most skilled archer, Hou-Yi, to help.

Hou-Yi aimed high and far. He shot down nine of the suns, and the world became safe again.

As a reward, Hou-Yi wanted the elixir of eternal life. But Hou-Yi was not a good man. He was cruel and wanted to live forever so that he could rule the people of China.

Since Hou-Yi had saved the world from becoming a desert, the Jade Emperor had no choice but to grant Hou-Yi his wish.

Hou-Yi's wife, Chang-E, knew of her husband's unkind ways. She took the elixir from Hou-Yi and ran away.

Hou-Yi chased Chang-E across the land, over rivers, valleys and mountains, until the harvest moon rose high above them.

Finally, with Hou-Yi at her back, Chang-E drank the elixir to escape and was lifted up to the moon, where she lives in the Jade Palace now and forever.

I look for Chang-E and the Jade Palace on the moon, but I don't see them. "Maybe they are on the other side," I say.

Mama and Baba smile and pull me close so I will stay warm.

“Time for mooncakes,” Mama says. We have mini ones and medium ones, but we share a big one. It tastes better when we eat it together.

Mama and Baba tell me about Wu-Gang, the woodcutter. He also lives on the moon.

Long ago, *a selfish woodcutter, Wu-Gang, wished to learn the secret of eternal life. He came upon an old hermit, who promised to teach him. In return, Wu-Gang would have to do exactly as the hermit said.*

Eager to live forever, Wu-Gang agreed.

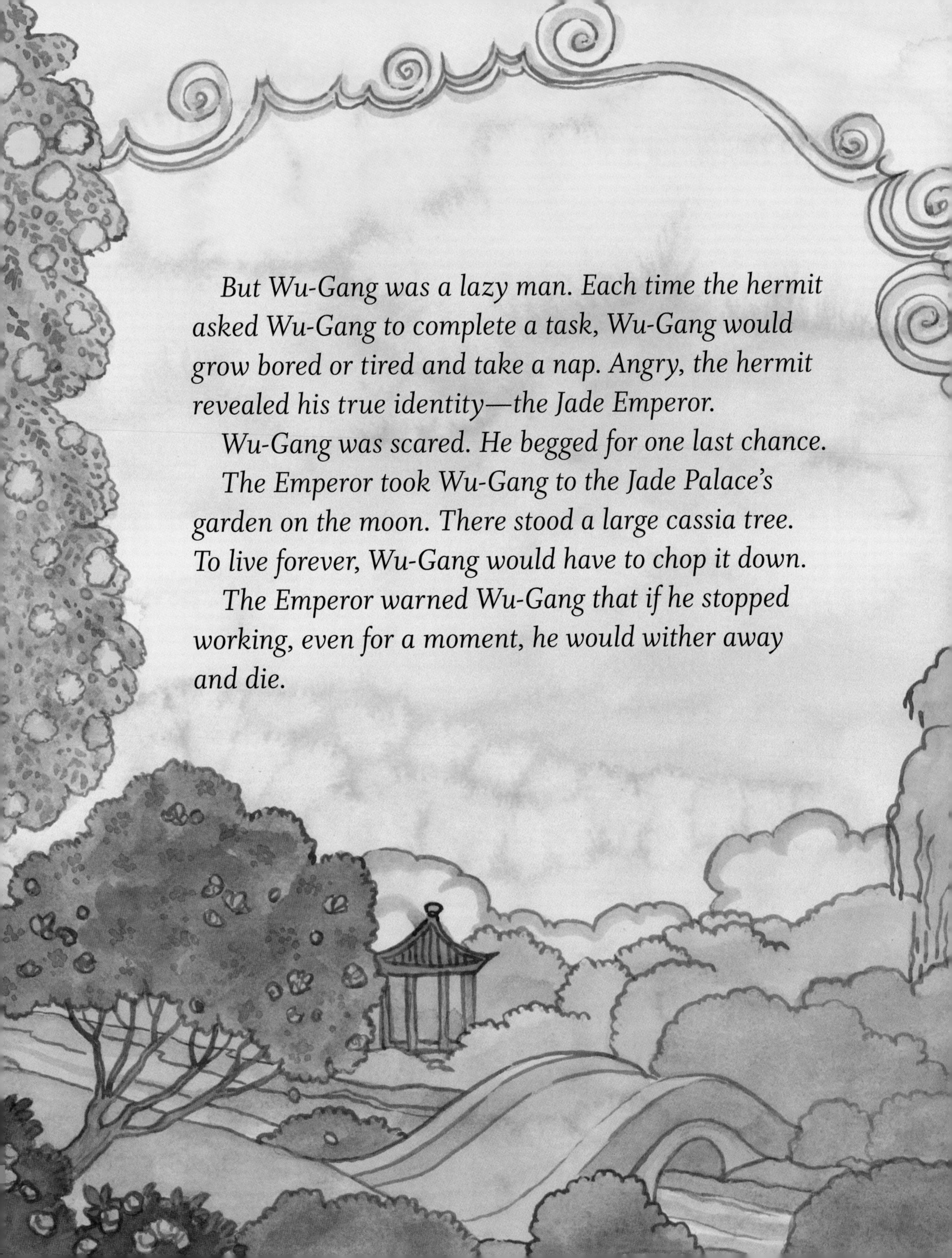

But Wu-Gang was a lazy man. Each time the hermit asked Wu-Gang to complete a task, Wu-Gang would grow bored or tired and take a nap. Angry, the hermit revealed his true identity—the Jade Emperor.

Wu-Gang was scared. He begged for one last chance.

The Emperor took Wu-Gang to the Jade Palace's garden on the moon. There stood a large cassia tree. To live forever, Wu-Gang would have to chop it down.

The Emperor warned Wu-Gang that if he stopped working, even for a moment, he would wither away and die.

Wu-Gang laughed at this simple job. He was a woodcutter, after all. But with each blow of his axe, the tree healed itself as though it had never been struck. Wu-Gang chopped and chopped, but the tree would not fall.

To this day, Wu-Gang is on the moon, still chopping and filling the air with the scent of cinnamon from the freshly cut cassia tree.

I look for Wu-Gang and the tree on the moon. But I don't see them. "I think I smell cinnamon," I say.

Mama and Baba smile, and Mama tweaks my nose.

"Time for tea," Baba says. He pours hot, steaming tea for us to drink. Mooncakes and tea are better than mooncakes alone.

Mama and Baba tell me about Jade Rabbit. Jade Rabbit lives on the moon too.

Long ago, three moon magicians wanted to test the goodness of the animals on earth. The magicians turned themselves into three poor old men and pretended to beg for food.

When they asked Fox, he gave them red berries from his den. When they asked Monkey, she gave them guavas pulled down from her tree. But when the moon magicians asked Rabbit, he had nothing to give.

Instead, Rabbit offered himself to the magicians for them to eat.

The three moon magicians were so amazed by Rabbit's kindness, they brought him back to the moon to live with them.

Rabbit became known as Jade Rabbit, and he still lives on the moon and brings food to those on earth who need it.

I look for Jade Rabbit on the moon, but I don't see him. "Does Jade Rabbit bring us mooncakes and tea too?" I ask, yawning.

Mama and Baba smile and press their cheeks against mine.

Eating mooncakes and lighting paper lanterns. Watching the round pearl moon and winking stars. Looking for Chang-E, Wu-Gang and Jade Rabbit. This is my Moon Festival. I can see Mama and Baba and me in the circle of the moon.

It's late. Mama and Baba say it's time to sleep. They hug me close. I blow out my lantern, and the smoke curls up to the sky.

"Thank you," I say to the moon before I go inside.

From my bedroom window, the moon watches over me. In my bed, I close my eyes and dream.

Author's Note

The Chinese Moon Festival falls on the fifteenth day of the eighth month of the lunar calendar. Traditionally, it is a time for families to come together and give thanks for the harvest and family unity. Even relatives who are unable to be with their families can look up at the dark sky and know that their loved ones are watching the same moon.